Magnificent Tales™

The Biggest and Toughest

The Short Story
of David's Big Faith

Based on 1 Samuel 17

Kelly Pulley

David C Cook

transforming lives together

THE BIGGEST AND TOUGHEST
Published by David C Cook
4050 Lee Vance View
Colorado Springs, CO 80918 U.S.A.

David C Cook Distribution Canada
55 Woodslee Avenue, Paris, Ontario, Canada N3L 3E5

David C Cook U.K., Kingsway Communications
Eastbourne, East Sussex BN23 6NT, England

The graphic circle C logo is a registered trademark of David C Cook.

LCCN 2012945762
ISBN 978-0-7814-0623-9
eISBN 978-1-4347-0587-7

Art and Text © 2012 Kelly Pulley

The Team: Susan Tjaden, Amy Konyndyk, Jack Campbell, Karen Athen

Manufactured in Hong Kong in October 2012 by Printplus Limited.
First Edition 2012

1 2 3 4 5 6 7 8 9 10

090512

For my dad, Robert Pulley,
the biggest and toughest

The Philistine army stood facing King Saul.
They acted as though they weren't frightened at all.
But King Saul's mighty army was shaking with fear,
falling over each other to get to the rear.

There, standing in front of the Philistine camp,
was a giant, the Philistines' fierce fighting champ!
His name was Goliath, and man was he scary!
His muscles were huge! His body was hairy!
He stood nine feet tall, 'bout as tall as a tree!
The biggest man anyone ever did see!
The men in Saul's army, and even King Saul,
thought he was the biggest and toughest of all!

The giant cried, "Send me a soldier to fight!
I'll smash him all day and I'll stomp him all night!
When all of the smashing and stomping is through,
your land will be ours … we'll make slaves out of you!"

For forty long days he repeated the call.
But no one would fight with him, no one at all.

Nearby, David, a shepherd boy, shepherded sheep,
keeping beasties away so his sheep he could keep.
Though three of his brothers had gone   h King Saul,
young David stayed home because he is too small.

His father gave David another big chore:
"Take food to your brothers out fighting the war."
Whatever his father would say, he'd obey,
so he packed up a donkey and went on his way.

When David arrived at the camp, he heard shouting—
mean insults and teases Goliath was spouting.

"Just when will you chickens send someone to fight?
I'll smash him all day and I'll stomp him all night!
When all of the smashing and stomping is through,
your land will be ours ... we'll make slaves out of you!"

Again the king's soldiers went running in fear,
falling over each other to get to the rear.

David called to the soldiers, "Hey, who is that dude?
His insults are mean! His teasing is rude!"
"Goliath!" they shouted, while running away.
"He's big and he's tough, you'd be silly to stay!"

But David decided to talk to King Saul,
to tell him that *he* was not frightened at all.
The king said, "Goliath is big and he's tough—
you're a boy with a sling, that's not nearly enough!"
Young David said, "I fought a lion and bear!
Both were bigger than I, so the fights were not fair.
With God as my strength both the beasts took a beating!
With God as my strength I will *not* be retreating!"

The king said to David, "The Lord be with you.
Take my sword and my shield, put my helmet on too."
But the armor was big and the sword weighed a lot.
They fit on the king, but on David ... did not.
So off came the armor and all the king's stuff.
"With God as my strength just my sling is enough!"

He gathered some stones from the bed of a stream.
As he did he could hear the big Philistine scream,
"I called for a soldier, you sent out a squirt!
Send him back to his mommy, he's gonna get hurt!
The boy is too puny to put up a fight!
I'll smash him all day and I'll stomp him all night!
When all of the smashing and stomping is through,
your land will be ours ... we'll make slaves out of you!"

Then David said, "You have your spear and your sword, but I will fight you *in the name of the Lord!*"

David loaded his sling and he spun it around.
The stone hit the giant ... then he hit the ground!

Now, the *Philistine* army went running in fear,
falling over each other to get to the rear.

Young David said, "*God* made the Philistine fall!
Because *God* is the biggest and toughest of all!"